For Granny Moose and Judith Morgan, with love

—David

For my nieces and nephews, the best school of fish I know,

except they aren't fish, just regular human kids

—Jared

Codzilla
Text copyright © 2019 by David Zeltser
Illustrations copyright © 2019 by Jared Chapman
All rights reserved. Manufactured in China.

www.harpercollinschildrens.com

Library of Congress Control Number: 2018943092
ISBN 978-0-06-257067-3

The artist used Adobe Photoshop to create the digital illustrations in this book, which was hard since he was underwater.
Design by Chelsea C. Donaldson
19 20 21 22 23 SCP 10 9 8 7 6 5 4 3 2 1

First Edition

CODZILLA

by **David Zeltser**
pictures by **Jared Chapman**

HARPER
An Imprint of HarperCollinsPublishers

Bertie was a big codfish.

VERY BIG.

When you are big, it's hard to fit in. And sometimes you don't know your own strength.

But Bertie was quite gentle, too. His favorite activity was reading in his school's library. He especially loved the books about sharks.

Maxwell was another cod in the school. His favorite activity was making Bertie's life miserable.

"Hey, everyone, look at the monster," he would say.

When Bertie would ask him to stop, Maxwell would always shout, "Hey, guys, what's this beast's name again?"

"CODZILLA!"
the other fish would reply.

And then they would laugh.

Bertie tried swimming away from Maxwell.

He tried hiding.

He even tried playing dead.

The fisherman comes at night

WHY WATER?

But nothing worked. Maxwell was always up in his gills.

So, one day, Bertie ate him.

Ah, thought Bertie, *that's the end of my problems.*

But Maxwell's buddies were on to him. "You're in big trouble, Codzilla!" they shouted.

So Bertie swallowed them, too.

"You can't just keep eating everyone!" said the school nurse.

"Mmmmmm," said Bertie. "School nurse."

Now I'll be one happy fish, he thought. He could finally read about sharks in peace.

Of course, it wasn't peaceful with all that bumping in his belly.

He needed a plan.

He read a book and got an idea.

He could make himself sneeze.

ACHOO!

ANCIENT

PREHISTORIC

He went to the ancient books section and opened the dustiest book he could find.

Dusty books make everyone sneeze!

"Sorry about that, guys," said Bertie, offering a fin of friendship.

"Get away from us, CODZILLA!" they all said.

Things were even worse now. Bertie started to cry.

Feeling empty, Bertie decided to leave his school forever.

"Help! Help!" came the sudden squeals.

The whole school was racing toward Bertie.

"SH-SH-SHARK!" cried Maxwell.

"We need somewhere to hide!"

"WHERE ARE THEY?"

demanded the shark.

"Hmmm–MMM?" mumbled Bertie.

"If I don't find those fish, I'm going to eat *you*, bones and all!"

Bertie showed him the book he was reading.

"Did you know that sharks have no bones?" he said.

"I'm boneless?" asked the shark.

Bertie nodded.

"Fine! But I can still sink my *teeth* into you."

"Did you know," said Bertie, "that sharks lose teeth when they eat?"

"Nice try, fish," growled the shark. "It's time to say goodbye!"

Bertie thought fast! "Isn't there *anything* else you want to know about sharks?"

The shark eyed the shelves. "Well," he whispered, "do you know anything about getting rid of shark breath? It's for a friend."

"I understand," said Bertie. "Take this, but you'd better get going—some sharks can't breathe if they stand still."

When the shark had gone, Bertie let loose!

Hooray!

Yes!

Splendid!

ACHOO!

As a reward for saving the school, Principal Crab awarded Bertie a very special title.

And no one ever called him Codzilla again.

From then on, that library had some **VERY BIG** borrowers.

And one very important rule:

NO EATING IN THE LIBRARY